YANKEE DOODLE

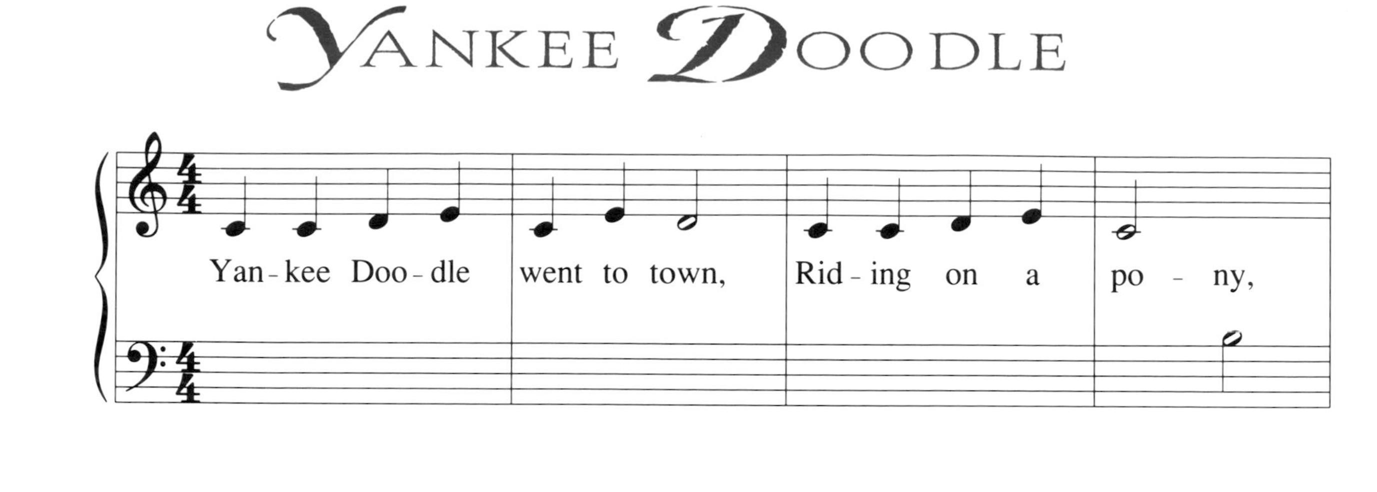

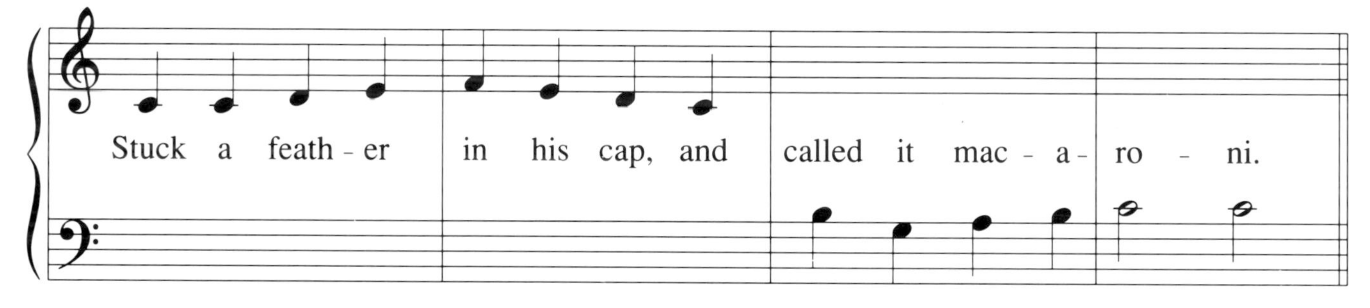

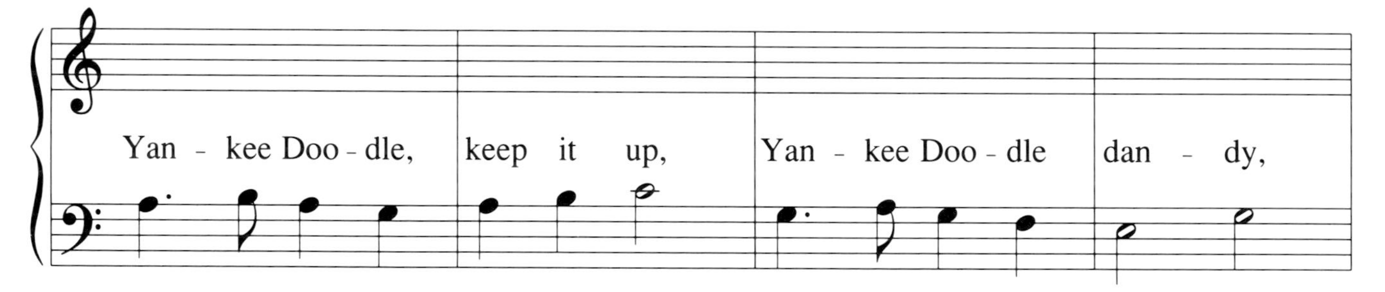

YANKEE DOODLE

YANKEE
STEVEN

Yankee Doodle

KELLOGG

Aladdin Paperbacks

First Aladdin Paperbacks edition June 1996

Aladdin Paperbacks
An imprint of Simon & Schuster
Children's Publishing Division
1230 Avenue of the Americas
New York, NY 10020

Also available in a Simon & Schuster
Books for Young Readers edition

The text of this book is set in 21-point Dutch 823.

Printed and bound in the United States of America

10 9 8 7 6 5 4 3 2 1

Library of Congress Cataloging-in-Publication Data
[Yankee Doodle]
Steven Kellogg's Yankee Doodle
p. cm.
Summary: An illustrated version of the well-known
song of the American Revolution.
ISBN 0-689-80158-0
1. Children's songs—United States—Texts. 2. United States—History—Revolution,
1775–1783—Songs and music. [1. Songs—United States. 2. United States—History—Revolution,
1775–1783—Songs and music.] I. Kellogg, Steven, ill. II. Title. III. Title: Yankee Doodle.
PZ8.3.B223Yan 1996 782.42164'0268—dc20 [E] 94-23603
0-689-80726-0 (Aladdin pbk.)

For Edward Tucker Jr.

Yankee Doodle went to town,
riding on a pony,

Stuck a feather in his hat
and called it macaroni.

Yankee Doodle, keep it up, Yankee Doodle dandy,
Mind the music and the step, and with the girls be handy.

Father and I went down to camp,
along with Captain Good'in,
And there we saw the men and boys
as thick as hasty puddin'.

And there we saw a thousand men
as rich as Squire David;

And what they wasted ev'ry day,
I wish it could be sav'ed.

Yankee Doodle, keep it up, Yankee Doodle dandy,
Mind the music and the step, and with the girls be handy.

And there I saw a little keg,
its head all made of leather,
They knocked on it with little sticks
to call the folks together.

And there was Captain Washington
upon a slapping stallion,
A-giving orders to his men—
I guess there was a million.

And the ribbons on his hat,
they looked so very fine, ah!
I wanted peskily to get
to give to my Jemima.

Yankee Doodle, keep it up, Yankee Doodle dandy,

Mind the music and the step, and with the...

And there I saw a swamping gun,
large as a log of maple.
Upon a mighty little cart—
a load for father's cattle.

And every time they fired it off,
it took a horn of powder,

It made a noise like father's gun,
only a nation louder!

The troopers, too, would gallop up
and fire right in our faces,

It scared me almost half to death
to see them run such races.

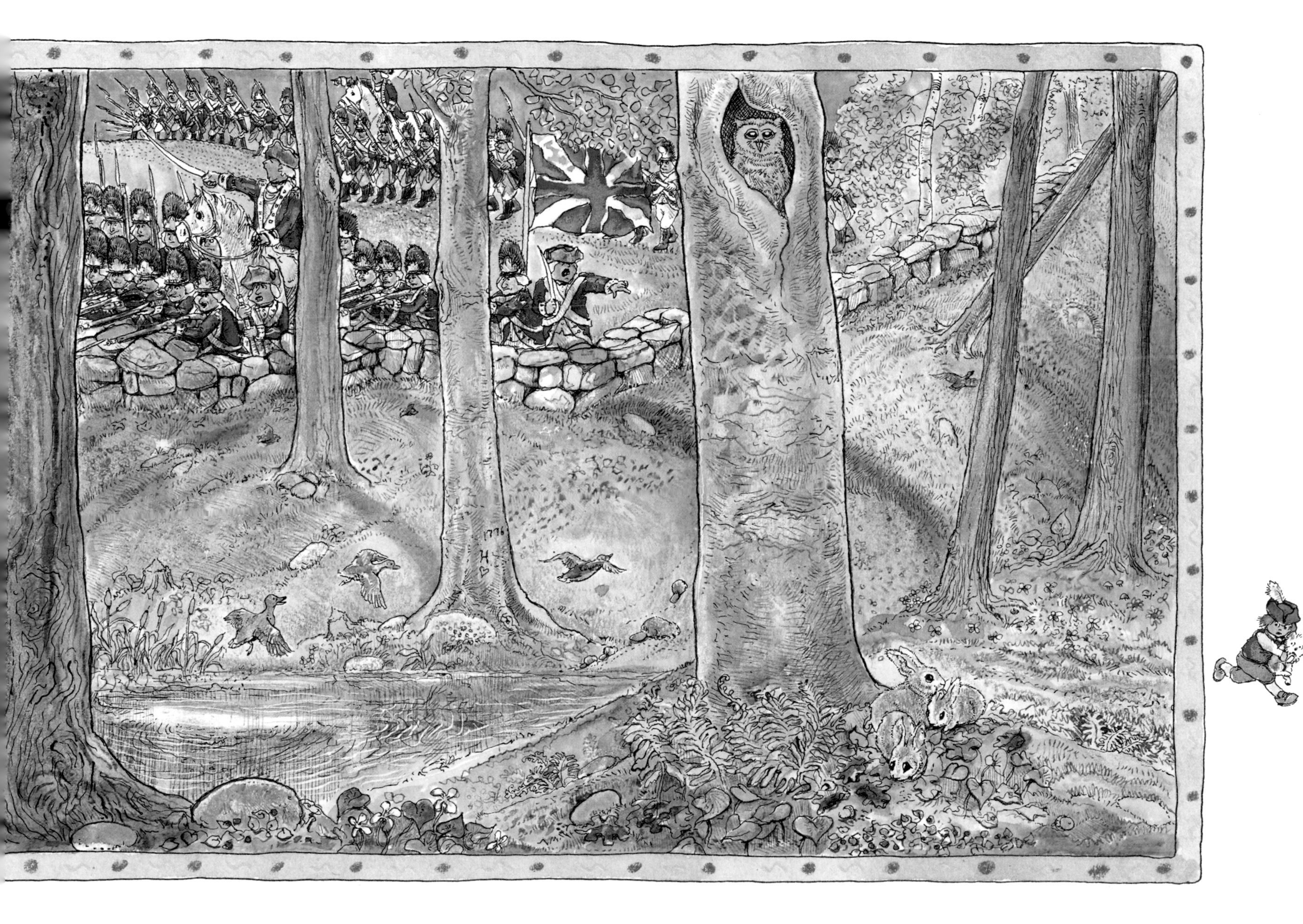

I saw another snarl of men,
a-digging graves, they told me,

So ’tarnal long, so ’tarnal deep,
they ’tended they should hold me.

It scared me so I hooked it off,
nor stopped, as I remember,

Nor turned about till I got home,
locked up in Mother's chamber.

Yankee Doodle, keep it up,

Yankee Doodle dandy,

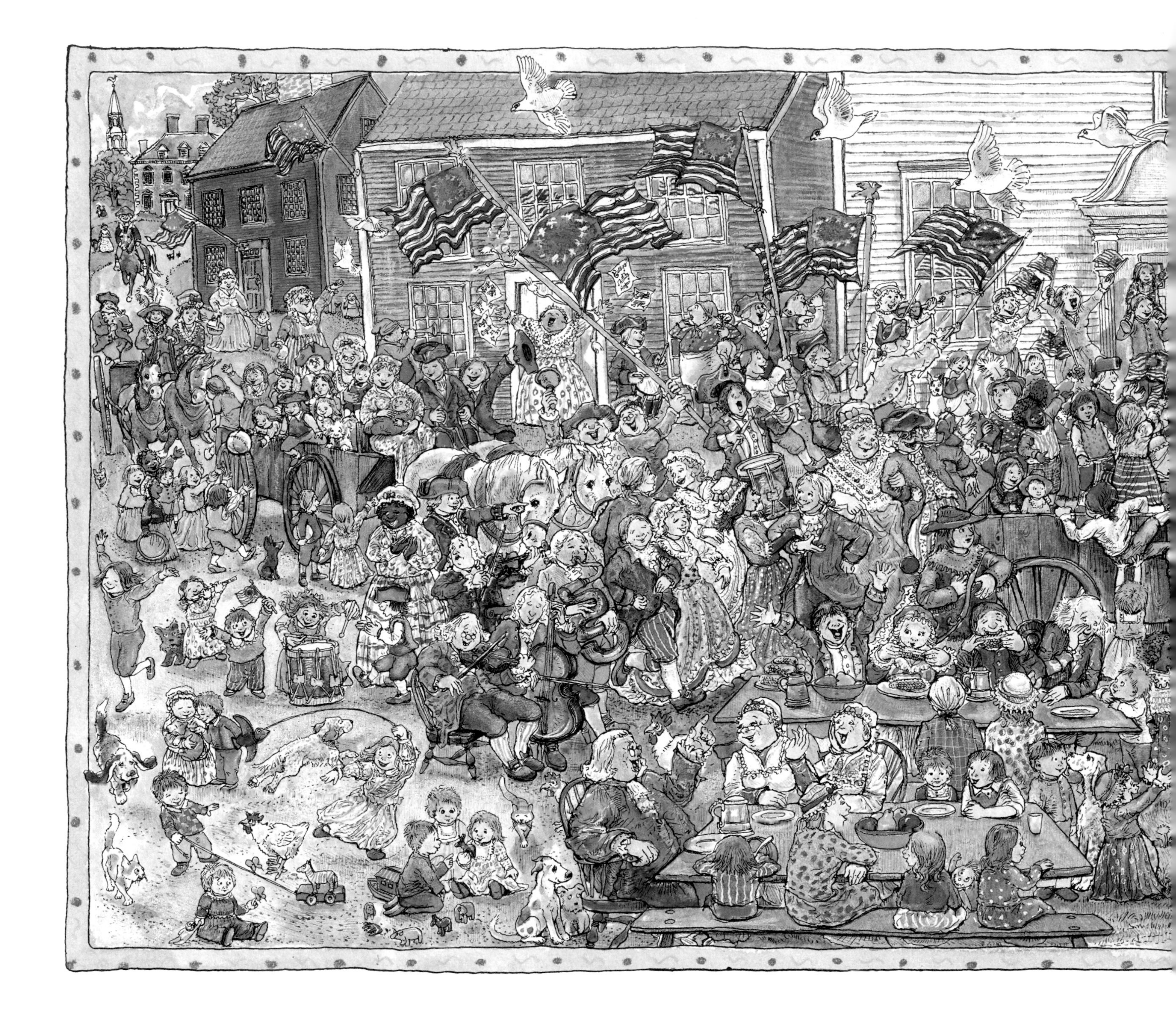

Mind the music and the step,

and with the girls be handy.

A Note About Yankee Doodle

Year after year, on the Fourth of July, generations of patriots in the United States parade to the high-spirited stanzas and chorus of *Yankee Doodle* in tribute to this country's struggle for independence during the Revolutionary War. But did you ever wonder exactly where the song came from? Who wrote it? And what it is all about?

Many people are surprised to hear that the tune was actually sung by the British at the beginning of the American Revolution (1775–1783) to poke fun at the colonists. (A "Yankee" is an old-fashioned name for people from New England, and the word "doodle" originally meant *to ridicule.)* Some attribute the song's authorship to Dr. Richard Shackburg, a surgeon in the British army, who may have heard several of the many variations of lyrics to a tune that had been sung in the colonies since the French and Indian War (1754–1763). When England's King George III sent his red-coated troops to make the colonists obey laws that they felt were unfair, it is said that the British bands played *Yankee Doodle*—mockingly, no doubt—as their ships arrived.

But in the nineteenth century, one musicologist declared that the song was definitely Yankee—not British—in its dialect, and he credited the song lyrics that we sing today to a member of the class of 1777 at Harvard College, Edward Bangs, who served as a minuteman at the Battle of Lexington during his sophomore year. Bangs may have rewritten the earlier Yankee song with a new hero, a naive and inquisitive young patriot, then printed it on a broadside as a rousing war song titled "The Yankee's Return from Camp." As the song's popularity grew, the American troops reclaimed it as their own, playing it triumphantly when the British general Cornwallis surrendered at Yorktown in 1781.

Even after the Revolutionary War ended, the jaunty tune just wouldn't go away. Not only was it again used as a battle song during the Mexican War (1846–1848) but it was also played and sung in theaters—and if the audiences didn't get to hear it, sometimes they called for it. The song was also borrowed for

The word "macaroni" did not always refer to just a type of pasta. It also meant a group of young, well-traveled Englishmen who often wore fancy trimmings on their hats and clothing. The trimming itself then became known as macaroni.

"Hasty puddin'" (pudding) is a thick porridge made of boiled water and flour, oatmeal, or cornmeal.

A "keg" is a small barrel—in this story, it is used as a makeshift musical instrument.

parodies and campaign jingles for politicians, including presidents William Henry Harrison, Zachary Taylor, and William Howard Taft. It is hard, then, to believe that a song with such history and adaptability has not changed at all since Edward Bangs's day. According to one source, the first and most popular verse may not have been added until twenty-four years after Bangs's death!

The mystery of the song's true authorship may never be fully solved. There are, to be sure, other lesser-known verses and variations of unknown origin, which you might find in different songbooks, such as:

And there they'd fife away like fun,
And play on cornstalk fiddles,
And some had ribbons red as blood,
All bound about their middles.

Uncle Sam came there to change
Some pancakes and some onions,
For 'lasses cake to carry home
To give his wife and young ones.

Yankee Doodle, doodle doo,
Yankee Doodle Dandy
All the lads and lasses are
As sweet as sugar candy.

The pictures in this book illustrate what might have happened to one proud colonial boy on the day that Captain George Washington took command of the rebel troops in Cambridge, Massachusetts, in July 1775. Edward Bangs himself may have witnessed this great event and—who knows?—it may have actually inspired him to reinvent what has become our foremost patriotic air, *Yankee Doodle*.

—STEVEN KELLOGG

Many of our nation's traditional songs have fascinating facts and stories behind them . . . check them out!

"Swamp" is a word that can mean "to beat or completely destroy," and in this story it refers to a powerful cannon ("swamping gun").

"'Tarnal" is an old-fashioned, local way of pronouncing "eternal," often used to mean "very."